# THE STORY OF DOCTOR DOLITTLE

## by HUGH LOFTING

# #6 Doctor Dolittle Goes Home

Adapted by Diane Namm

Illustrated by John Kanzler

STERLING

New York / London

www.sterlingpublishing.com/kids

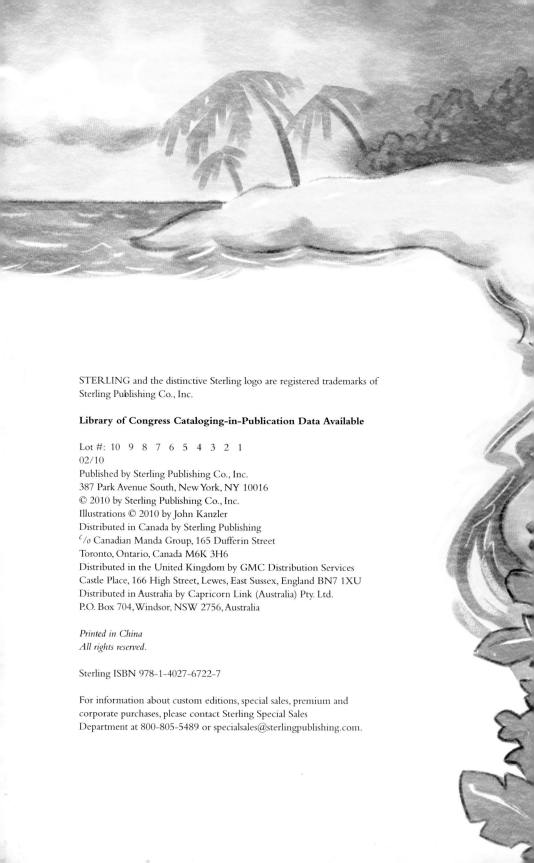

STERLING and the distinctive Sterling logo are registered trademarks of
Sterling Publishing Co., Inc.

**Library of Congress Cataloging-in-Publication Data Available**

Lot #: 10  9  8  7  6  5  4  3  2  1
02/10
Published by Sterling Publishing Co., Inc.
387 Park Avenue South, New York, NY 10016
© 2010 by Sterling Publishing Co., Inc.
Illustrations © 2010 by John Kanzler
Distributed in Canada by Sterling Publishing
$^c$/o Canadian Manda Group, 165 Dufferin Street
Toronto, Ontario, Canada M6K 3H6
Distributed in the United Kingdom by GMC Distribution Services
Castle Place, 166 High Street, Lewes, East Sussex, England BN7 1XU
Distributed in Australia by Capricorn Link (Australia) Pty. Ltd.
P.O. Box 704, Windsor, NSW 2756, Australia

*Printed in China*
*All rights reserved.*

Sterling ISBN 978-1-4027-6722-7

For information about custom editions, special sales, premium and
corporate purchases, please contact Sterling Special Sales
Department at 800-805-5489 or specialsales@sterlingpublishing.com.

# Contents

# An Unexpected Guest

Doctor Dolittle sailed for home.

"We're done with adventures from now on,"
he said.

"We found Circus Crocodile's mother,
we cured King Lion's prince cub,
and we left the pirates far behind us.
It will be smooth sailing from here on."

Just then they heard a
knock-knock-knock.

"What in the world can that be?"
Doctor Dolittle wondered.
Everyone searched the ship,
inside and out, above and below.

Then, to everyone's surprise,
a door in the deck opened
and out popped a little boy!
"Who are you?" Doctor Dolittle asked.

"Who are you?" asked the boy.
"And where are the pirates?" he added
as he climbed up onto the deck.

"How did you get on this ship?"
Doctor Dolittle asked.
"I thought it would be fun
to be a pirate," the little boy said.

"But the pirates were mean,"

the boy explained,

"so I hid down below."

"Where are you from?"

Doctor Dolittle asked.

"I don't know the name,"
the little boy said.

"But I know it's that way," he pointed.

"Or maybe it's this way," he added.

Doctor Dolittle did not know
what to do. How could he
return the little boy home if
he didn't know which way to go?

Doctor Dolittle gave a squeak, a whistle, and two short honks, and a family of dolphins swam up to the ship.

"Tell me," Doctor Dolittle said
to the oldest and wisest dolphin.
"Dolphins always know
what is happening at sea.
Which island is this boy from?"
"No idea," the dolphin squeaked.

## A Nosy Dog

Doctor Dolittle paced up
and down the ship's deck.
"Think, my boy," the doctor said.
"Did you bring anything from home?"
The little boy thought for a minute.
"I've got this," he said.

He reached into his pocket and
held up a tiny scrap of food.
"My mother made this for me.
This is all that is left."

Jip the dog sniffed the food.

"Mmmm," barked Jip.

"I've smelled that spice before.

Go that way."

Jip pointed with his nose.

"That yummy smell comes from there."

## The Stowaway Returns

Doctor Dolittle turned the boat
to follow the tip of Jip's nose.
They sailed for hours.
It seemed as if they might
never find the little boy's home.
"Look!" the little boy shouted.
He dived off the ship's deck and swam
all the way to shore right into…

… his mother's waiting arms.

"Wait for me!" barked Jip.

"Me too!" snorted the pushmi-pullyu.

"Me three!" quacked Dab-Dab.

"And me!" Gub-Gub oinked.

"A thousand thanks," the mother said.

She hugged her little boy tight.

"How can I ever repay you?"

She gave the doctor a big kiss!

Doctor Dolittle turned bright red.
He didn't know what to say.
"I'm hungry," said the little boy.
"So are we!" the animals agreed,
and they all helped themselves to
big bowls of hot soup.

"This calls for a celebration,"
the doctor declared.
"Let's have a parade!"
Dab-Dab quacked.

"I just love a good parade,"
the pushmi-pullyu said.
The little boy stood up.
"Follow me!" he cried.

Everyone had a wonderful time
in the parade.
They marched here and there,
all around, until finally
the good doctor said,
"time for us to go!

My sister will be wondering where
we have been these long months."
"We understand,"
the little boy said sadly.

After many hugs and kisses
and quite a few tears,
Doctor Dolittle and the animals
were at long last ready to leave.

# Home At Last

Doctor Dolittle and the animals
headed for home.
After many days at sea
they finally spotted
the Puddleby shore.
Happy and excited, the animals
jumped up and down.
"I wonder if things have changed,"
Doctor Dolittle said. "Or perhaps
things will be exactly the same!"

Doctor Dolittle's house
was exactly the same.
There were bills piled high
and the floor was dusty.

Doctor Dolittle's sister walked in.
"Oh, my!" she exclaimed when she saw
the pushmi-pullyu in the hall. "I've never
seen such an amazing creature before!"

"His wool grows like magic,"
Doctor Dolittle explained.
"If only we had some magic
to make our bills go away."

"Magic wool!" his sister said.

There was a twinkle in her eyes.

"I'll knit sweaters for everyone.

Then we will be just fine!"

Things were different after that.
Doctor Dolittle's sister knitted
sweaters and sold them
to everyone in Puddleby.
The bills were paid. The house
was clean. The animals had
sweaters. And there was
always a lot to eat.
Doctor Dolittle cared for
all the animals in town.
And everyone lived happily—
and warmly—ever after.